A shop full of

KITTENS

Ian Penney

G. P. Putnam's Sons • New York

For Mum, Dad, Polly and Fanny

Also illustrated by Ian Penney
(Verse by Kevin Crossley-Holland)
Under the Sun and Over the Moon

Text and illustrations copyright © 1990 by Ian Penney. All rights reserved.
This book, or parts thereof, may not be reproduced
in any form without permission in writing from the publisher.
First American edition published in 1991 by G. P. Putnam's Sons, a division of
The Putnam & Grosset Book Group, 200 Madison Avenue, New York, NY 10016.
Originally published in 1990 by Orchard Books, London. Printed in Belgium.

Library of Congress Cataloging-in-Publication Data
Penney, Ian.   A shop full of kittens / Ian Penney. – 1st American ed.   p.   cm.
Summary: Tabitha Cat ventures from her home in the basement of a department
store to find her kittens who are hiding throughout the store.
[1. Cats – Fiction.   2. Hide-and-seek – Fiction.
3. Department stores – Fiction.] I. Title.
PZ7.P3848Sh 1991 [E] – dc20 90-8939 CIP AC
ISBN 0-399-22280-4

1 3 5 7 9 10 8 6 4 2

First American edition

Tabitha Cat lived in a department store. Her home was in the basement, where she took care of her nine kittens.

She liked to prowl around the store when it was open and keep an eye on things, while the kittens stayed safely tucked away in a basket in the basement.

POLLY

When the store was closed, Tabitha Cat let the kittens go out to play. They loved exploring and playing hide-and-seek in different departments.

GEORGE

Tabitha Cat didn't mind where the kittens went,
as long as they were back home again by opening time.

THOMAS

LUCY

SALLY

BILLY

FLORENCE

But one morning the kittens
didn't want to come home.
It was much more fun
playing games among the
potted plants and the carpets,
the china and the jewelry, and all the
other wonderful things for sale in the store.

TOBY

PETER

Tabitha Cat was very cross with those naughty kittens. And she set off to find them and bring them home.

First she went to the fish counter in the food department.

"I wonder if Polly's here," she said. "She likes fish. Perhaps she's behind the salmon on the top shelf?" Or is she near the shellfish on the bottom shelf?"

"Polly, I can see your little black nose," said Tabitha Cat.

"Come here at once."

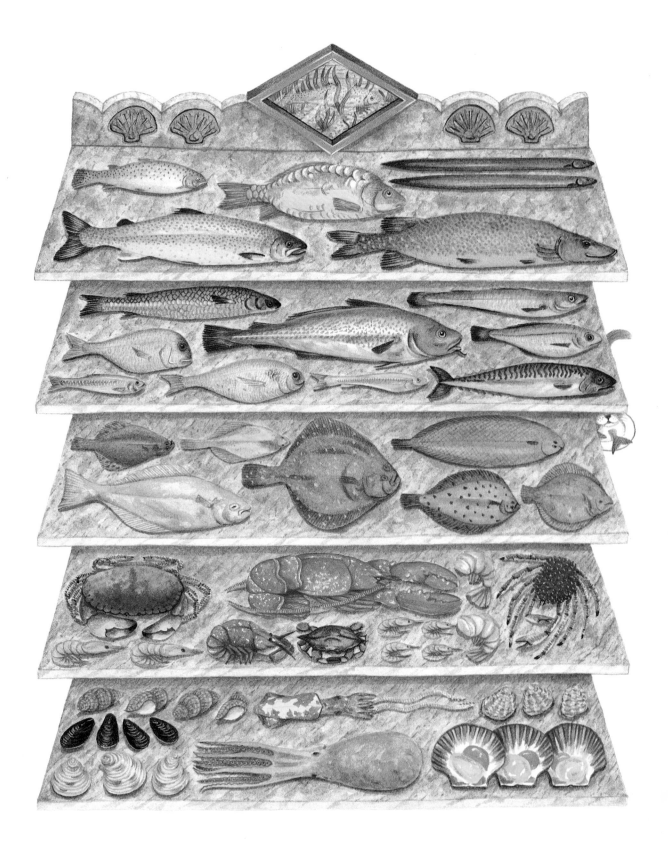

Out jumped Polly, and together they looked through the rest of the food department.

"If I know George," said Tabitha Cat, "he'll be hiding here too — near the apples and bananas, or the cookies and cakes, or the coffee, or the cheese…

"There you are!" she said. "Come along with me, George."

George and Polly
followed their mother to
the clothing department.
   A kitten could be hiding
anywhere – under a hat,
wrapped in a scarf, inside a
boot, behind a big, bright tie.
   "I can see you, Lucy," said Tabitha Cat.
"Come along with
your brother and sister."

Then Tabitha Cat took Lucy, George, and Polly along to the music department.

Was there a kitten hiding under the piano, behind the cello, or near the guitar or the big bass drum?

Yes there was!

"I can see Toby's ears peeping out," said Tabitha Cat. "Come out of there!"

Then Toby, Lucy, George, and Polly ran to look among the clocks and furniture.

High up on the grandfather clock, six mice were playing hickory-dickory-dock.

There was a kitten somewhere too…

"You can't hide from me, Sally," said Tabitha Cat. "Out you come!"

Sally, Toby, Lucy, George, and Polly
skipped along behind Tabitha Cat to the
kitchenwares department.

There were pots and pans, ladles and
spoons, whisks, jugs, kettles and bowls…

"I can see you, Billy," said Tabitha Cat.

"Hurry up now."

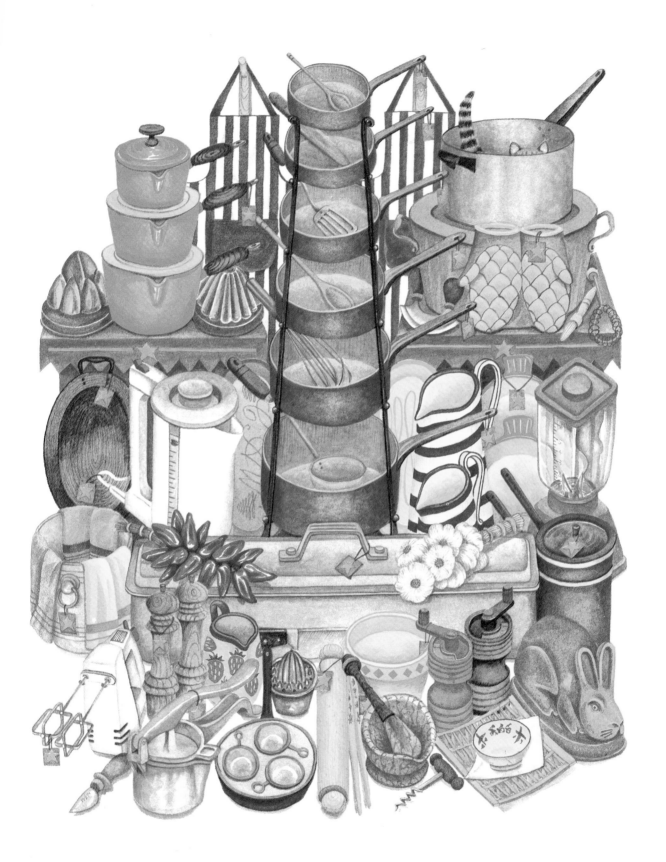

Tabitha Cat marched Billy, Sally, Toby, Lucy, George, and Polly to the garden department.

Who could be hiding behind the pretty flowers and the potted plants? "Hurry up, Florence; no time for games," said Tabitha Cat.

Florence, Billy, Sally, Toby, Lucy, George, and Polly scampered along behind their mother to the toy department – the kittens' favorite place.

There was a dollhouse and a sailboat, a rag doll and three teddy bears.

"I can see Thomas," squeaked Florence.

"Come along, Thomas," said Tabitha Cat.

"It's nearly opening time."

One, two, three, four, five, six, seven,
eight kittens. Look where they had been hiding!
Polly was nibbling scraps under the fish
counter, George was behind an orange
pumpkin, Lucy was under a hat with a big
brim, Toby was inside a shiny tuba, Sally
was playing roly-poly in a rug. Billy
was hiding in a saucepan,

Florence had jumped
into a pot of daffodils,
and Thomas was ready
to sail across the sea.

But Tabitha Cat had nine kittens.
Where was Peter?

Peter was curled up in the basket,
fast asleep. Tabitha Cat purred happily.
All nine kittens were back in the
basement, safe and sound.

It was time for the store to open.